Kit

D1168135

Saw this &
thought of
you!

Jamie

TALES TO READ
ALOUD
TO YOUR CAT

Mario Sartori

TALES TO READ ALOUD TO YOUR CAT

Volume 1:
Tiger

Illustrations by
Donald Sanders

E. P. DUTTON   NEW YORK

Published in the United States by E. P. Dutton,
a division of NAL Penguin Inc.,
2 Park Avenue, New York, N.Y. 10016.

Published simultaneously in Canada
by Fitzhenry and Whiteside, Limited, Toronto.

Library of Congress Cataloging-in-Publication Data
Sartori, Mario.
   Tales to read aloud to your cat / Mario Sartori; illustrations by Donald Sanders. — 1st ed.
      p.   cm.
   Contents: v. 1. Tiger.
   ISBN 0-525-24717-3
   1. Cats—Fiction.   I. Sanders, Donald (Donald Lee)   II. Title.
PS3569.A74T35   1988   813'.54—dc19   88-14976

Designed by Steven N. Stathakis

10 9 8 7 6 5 4 3 2 1

First Edition

This story is dedicated to George, *of course, and to Peggy and George, who so wisely brought him into my life.*

TALES TO READ ALOUD TO YOUR CAT

George was not a country cat, in fact, he was *very much* a city cat and proud of it. As a result, he was more than a little disturbed when Howie—the man he lived with—decided to move to a farm.

There are city cats and there are *city cats* but George took an absolute delight in everything about his life there. He seemed made to live in vast, high ceilinged apartments overlooking the park, relishing the time he spent looking from the huge windows down at the changing patterns of people and cars. He would gaze for hours as the buildings first reflected the sun's light and then later glowed on through the night, powered from within.

To George, the skyline and the traffic were friends whom he checked in with every day. He was born there among them; it was his home, his birthright. He loved his life. He certainly would miss it but he realized there wasn't much he could do about the move. The thought of running away from home never entered his mind because he sensed that somehow the city could be a very different place close up from what it appeared to be from his window. More importantly he loved the man more than any of these other things.

So the day actually did arrive when Howie packed George into the backseat of their new station wagon. Can you imagine? thought George. The car symbolized everything strange and new about the move. It was the most impractical of cars in the city, an impediment to travel in fact, of no real use, yet here was Howie saying that they'd be lost without it on the "farm," as he now loved to call their new home.

George was getting more than a little tired of hearing about the wonders of *the farm*. He'd been hearing little else for the last few months as friends were told about each step in finding, acquiring and redoing *the farm*.

Many of these friends mirrored George's own objections to the move. "Howie, what do you know about the country or a farm?" "Where would you work?" "Where is the closest *decent* restaurant?" "Are you crazy giving up *this* apartment?" But each question was answered, explained or shrugged off and that was all there was to it. They were moving—TODAY.

The thing was that Howie was really *city people* too—didn't he realize that! Did he think that all of his problems were going to disappear merely by planting his feet firmly in dirt? It made George furious to think about it. Actually he felt sorry for Howie. This had been a very hard year for him. He had

had to face the fact that he was almost forty and not only presently alone but, despite the large number of friends he had, quite likely to remain single forever. The forever part was probably what had brought about the idea of *a change*.

Now George was actually lying on the backseat of this annoying station wagon, not saying a word—but there was no mistaking the fact that he was *most* displeased. He tried to imagine the wagon filled with hay or pens of rabbits; he couldn't conjure up any other images of what people did in the country, much less in a station wagon. After all, he had only seen *Seven Brides for Seven Brothers* once. On the other hand, Howie sat up front and never stopped talking. An obvious attempt to mask nervousness, George thought, but since he was feeling far from understanding at the moment he decided that Howie deserved all of the problems that his stupid decision would bring him. So he kept quite to himself.

George concentrated on looking out at the other cars, most of them a much more sensible size and fashionable shape than theirs, and at the buildings. The cars and the buildings were becoming scarce, replaced by large trees and small houses. In time George saw trucks and vans instead of the city cars and he began to realize that this was for real and that he might never see his beloved city again. He left the car seat and climbed in back to perch on some boxes and look out through the rear gate at the highway that was taking them farther and farther from home. Cats don't normally cry, but George heaved several deep sighs as he hunched in the back of that station wagon.

It seemed hours later when they actually arrived at the farm. This was not a "farm" farm—eighty-foot silos, mighty herds and field after field. Howie wasn't that silly. No, in real-estate-agent talk, we're talking a "charming" old house on about twenty acres of mostly wooded land. There was a small barn with, at the moment, a handful of animals the previous owners had "gladly" left behind as part of the deal. There was also a large kitchen garden and a rather pathetic hilly field that Howie vowed he would keep mowed and "neat-looking" at all costs. This was what George saw as the car pulled up in front of his new home, a city person's idea of a farm—neat, clean and controllable.

As soon as they arrived, Howie came to the back of the car, let down the gate and picked George up to carry him inside. George had to admit it, Howie did take proper care of him, not that he didn't deserve it. Since he was six weeks old, he had given the best years of his life to his friend. That was ten years ago, and he was showing no adverse signs of age. No, he was a mature cat. That's how George viewed himself— "mature," at his best, looking forward to many fruitful years. If only Howie hadn't gotten this silly idea that the country was going to be the answer to all of his fears and problems—that is would erase all doubts about the future. To him, the country was *the* answer; to George it was just one big question mark!

Surprisingly, George liked the house at once. He was relieved to see and smell so much of the wonderful old furniture he had grown up with in the apartment. He settled on a familiar chair and was astonished to see how different things appeared in these surroundings. The light was different here; that is what he noticed the most. The sun filtered down into the room through newly emerging green leaves and then bounced off the honey-colored walls and the golden oak woodwork. It was nearly spring. There was the feeling of sunlight trapped underwater and floating lazily, heavily. This

made the room look so warm that, in spite of himself, George began to feel comfortable.

Though still unsettled and angry about the move, George was a conscientious cat and quite a talkative cat. So muttering and meowing each step of the way, he began to investigate every square inch of the house. Have you ever seen a cat take possession of a new place where he will live? Well, mainly he inspects it to make sure that there are no dangers there that humans have overlooked. Humans tend to be rather casual about such things and that is why many of them have the good sense to invite cats into their homes to look after the important details. Even by cat standards George was thorough in these matters. He examined room after room, looking into cupboards and closets, behind shower curtains and drapes, and at last he climbed the wide plank steps to the attic.

The attic was different from anyplace that George had ever been before. It was so much "older" than the apartment, even older than the rest of this house. That of course was impossible, he knew, but downstairs everything had been stripped and cleaned and painted so often and so recently that the old raw boards of the attic seemed ancient by comparison. There were two windows up here, both with nice wide sills where George knew he would spend much of his time. One looked out toward the back of the house and had a view of fields and the barn and, if you looked straight down, you could see the roof of the little back porch.

The other window looked out toward the road and the front yard with its two enormous trees. He sat for a while and sampled the view from each sill. Looking out at the deserted barnyard, George sensed the presence of other animals nearby—frightened, confused, questioning.

George closed his eyes, stretching his head toward the warm spring sunlight as it poured through the window. He realized that he would spend many days sitting just like this in the warmth and light. Yes, the attic was definitely his favorite part of the house. It was warm, because that's the way attics are, but it was also "real," as if in this place the house was still allowed to be most itself, most alive without interference from men. And George felt that the house was good, and welcomed them and was willing to put up with the silly renovation and decoration because it was happy to again have people to look after. George liked that and began to purr contentedly rubbing and scratching his face against the rough corner of the window ledge. This is real country living, he thought dreamily.

When George finally went back downstairs he found his food on the floor in the kitchen where Howie was cooking dinner, then he went into the parlor where a fire had been built in the fireplace. He lay next to the hearth and began to wash himself but all the while he kept one eye on the flames. The fire fascinated George. In the city they hadn't had a *real* fireplace. Oh, they had that big marble one, but it didn't work and so George had ignored it except for a period when as a kitten he loved to hide behind things on the mantel and leap out at Howie, as he passed by, to surprise him. It had been his favorite game for a while. But that was a long time ago, and this fireplace was very different.

George studied the leaping flames and the bed of glowing cinders. The whole scene reminded him of the city as it looked from the windows of the apartment. The flames were like the tall buildings bathed in their own light, and the crackling-glowing cinders were like the nightly patterns of traffic in the streets. It was with this picture in mind that he dozed off.

Much later, when he awoke, he found that Howie had gone upstairs and that he was alone. The house was very quiet. He listened to the sounds of the country and he heard the house most of all, breathing and sighing through its floors and chimneys. He heard murmurs of the animal life outside and the man's steady breathing upstairs. All were good sounds, and he felt at home. He missed the city but being a mature cat he would give this place a chance. What other choice did he have anyway? Upstairs he settled on the new quilt, happy that it felt as warm and soft as the old one always had. He fell back to sleep quickly. His first day in the country had turned out better than he had imagined it would.

In total darkness, George awoke suddenly, his body tensed. As he fought to focus his senses, his jaw distended into an enormous yawn. There was something in the house, moving. He heard it, and it wasn't a person. It wasn't a thief, it was an animal—somewhere. George sprang off the bed and listened at the opened door, his head cocked and his claws ready. Whatever it was was *upstairs*. He was up the attic stairs in a second.

He wasn't used to stairs and was surprised at how fast he had made the run. The attic was dark now, the evening had turned cloudy and there was very little moonlight coming through the windows. George remained poised on the top step of the stairway, slowly surveying the room. It took several seconds until, in the corner, not far from the front window, he was able to make out the small bent shape of a squirrel.

It was bleeding. He could sense that from here. The animal was looking at him with a look that combined fear, despair and anger all at once. George wasn't sure what he should do. He certainly wasn't afraid of a squirrel, but what was it doing in his attic? And the blood, what about that? He crept closer. The squirrel tensed noticeably as George approached.

It was dying. George saw that more and more clearly as he grew near. He heard the forced breathing, now reduced to gasps, and he could now make out a gaping wound in its heaving chest. The small animal had been bleeding heavily, and a small puddle of blood had formed under it on the attic floor. George felt great pity as he approached the cowering figure. Had it been struck by a car? No, cars don't tear an animal like that. This animal had been harmed in a far more brutal and deliberate way.

George didn't know what to do. He felt powerless, the same way he felt when he would come upon Howie crying alone. He could feel how much the squirrel needed help, but

all he could do was to stay near, hoping that that was enough, that it would make a difference. He crouched down as close to it as he could get and began to purr deeply, hoping that the soothing sound might help. The squirrel seemed to relax slightly, but the pain was still heavily etched on its sharp features. George shifted his position slightly to avoid the widening pool of blood.

It was then that the squirrel spoke, very weakly, in a voice that wasn't much louder than the rustle of the nearby trees. "The dog did this—watch out for the dog." The word *dog* was prolonged, it sounded like a cry for help—a cry against.

George was flustered, and when cats are flustered they often just for a split second mind you, become almost human. It's amazing how silly they can sound. "I don't go outside, I'll probably never see the dog. I'm sure the man will do something about it. He's very careful about things. Why, in the city we had an exterminator come every other week. You know it wasn't our dog. We've never had one because you have to take them out for walks and in the city it's just too much bother. Once Howie's sister was going away and we had to take care of her two Irish setters, Toby and. . . ." The squirrel glared at him through eyes that were fast becoming slits. "NO," he hissed. "The wild dog—he's everywhere—he can get everywhere." "Well he's not coming here, not to my house!" George was surprised at how possessive he felt about the matter. He was also happy to be back in control. The squirrel panted and made an odd gurgling sound as it spoke. "The animals—he'll come, you'll see—he'll kill your animals, you'll see, when nobody's there, he'll get them one by one. They are *your* animals. Protect your animals from the dog," and then he died.

George had seen roaches die. It often happened after he had been playing with them, but surely there was no connection between the two. But this animal died because it was torn and hurt. George didn't like this at all. He inched closer to the squirrel and again began to purr. Though he knew it was dead he felt that he should continue to keep it company—at least for a little while. So George kept his vigil. A thin ray of moonlight illuminated the squirrel and the now quiet ruby pool that had formed, framing his little body. George began

to think about the squirrels he had seen in the city. From the apartment windows, high above the trees, they looked like ants, without color or interest. At least the birds could fly and often came near the windows and offered a little diversion, but the squirrels were nothing but a sense of random movement down near the pavement. Being so close to one now made George realize that he hadn't been correct about them in the past. They were much more catlike than he had dreamed.

After an hour or so George went down to get Howie. It was easy to awaken him. George walked across his chest, and when this didn't work he put his head under Howie's chin and began to push upward. In no time Howie was tossing about and grumbling but very much awake. George began to meow now and to walk back and forth between the bed and the bedroom door. Complaining that it wasn't time for George to eat yet, Howie nevertheless got out of bed and stumbled into the hall after him. He intended to fill up George's dish anyway, and then hopefully be allowed several more hours of sleep before morning. Partly right, thought George as he brushed against Howie every step of the way to give him encouragement. As soon as they reached the middle of the hallway George went to the attic stairs and crouched there emitting a sound much closer to a growl than a meow. That caught your attention, George thought, as he saw Howie turn and regard him with a look of amazement. George led the way and Howie followed. The fact is, people are basically intelligent if you give them a chance.

George brought him upstairs to where the squirrel lay, and then looked up at the man. Howie was clearly amazed. The idea that George was responsible for this flickered across his mind. It's very easy to see what people are thinking. They are so unlike a cat. But George quickly by several movements and thoughts of concern let Howie realize how absurd that notion was. Shaking his head over the scene, Howie bent closer to examine the squirrel, then he picked George up and carried him downstairs, closing the attic door tightly behind them.

The next morning Howie was up and working before George woke. The attic door was again open and the squirrel was gone. George could smell the fresh earth on Howie's shoes and felt happy knowing that the animal had been properly buried. While he ate, Howie discussed the dog situation with a neighbor on the telephone. He had been warned about it by the former owners and this morning was deciding the best way to destroy it in order to protect the outdoor animals. George was pleased with the conversation. The man would handle this and there would be no more incidents. So much for the dog. He jumped up on the window seat in the warm, soft sunlight and he began to clean himself.

If the truth were to be known, George didn't really like dogs under the best of circumstances. In the city every other apartment seemed to have one and you'd hear them all day long yapping at every little sound in the hall or pacing the floor waiting for their walks, or for their food, or for this or that. Dogs are so helpless, he thought, so dependent. He didn't like them at all. Arrested development. Yes, dogs are like children, he thought, dependent and demanding at the same time. They grab for what they want, or think they want, with no regard to consequences—spoiled children. He thought again of the poor squirrel now neatly out of sight; you could count on Howie for that.

As he cleaned himself, he also kept an eye on the man, who was now out in the yard working near the barn. The barn interested George for the same reasons that the attic did—not too much had been done to it over the years to make it into anything other than what it had been built to be. Pushing open the screen door George decided to go outside and have a better look. George had never walked on dirt before, and he immediately liked the cool feeling against the pads of his paws. He also liked the smell of the grasses and the flowers out here. But as he approached the barn he was definitely not ready for the smell of the various animals that hit him all at once. Howie was surprised to see him outside. It was funny to see the look of panic quickly leave Howie's face when he suddenly realized that there were no cars or trucks or crazy neighbors that could do George harm. Howie came over and picked him up, carrying him into the barn to "introduce" him to the animals.

George looked around very cautiously, his body stiff, even though he was in the man's arms. Cats look out for themselves, always aware that humans aren't completely reliable. These animals were BIG! To begin with there was the horse; George recognized that from the various horses he had seen pulling carriages into the park. Close up a horse was enormous! Looking into his eyes George immediately knew that it was a good animal, very tired, but kind and sweet, an animal that could be trusted. Now, the goat was another matter. Oh, what a smell! The goat was high-strung and nasty, suspicious and unfriendly; he was immediately resentful that George was here and that the man was holding him. No, thought George, this goat is not worth knowing even if I could learn to ignore the smell.

There were also white things, furry, big, skittish, musty-smelling white things, and there were a lot of them. Well, maybe not a lot; there were five. Three big ones and two little ones. One was really small and not too steady on its feet. Howie called them sheep. He brought George close to the pen where they all huddled together. They actually gave off a scent of fear, a scent that reminded George a little of the squirrel that he would have rather forgotten. Close up the sheep looked interesting; they appeared to be so soft, probably it would be easy to wash them so that they would be white and shining. A cat looks for cleanliness wherever possible. The problem with the sheep was that they smelled so, and were so afraid that George couldn't imagine that they would ever make stimulating companions. Howie put George down on the straw in the middle of the barn floor. Not much choice, thought George, and he sprang up to the rail around the horse's stall.

From up there George looked down on the other animals. Though there really weren't that many of them it still seemed crowded in the small barn. As he watched, Howie led the goat outside and tied him to a post in the barnyard. Then he came back in and did his best to lead the sheep out to a patch of grassy land beside the horse's paddock. Howie didn't really know how to get their attention, and they were so frightened to begin with that George had to smile as they all stumbled into each other and almost pinned the man against the doorframe in their mad scramble to do what they felt was expected of them. Sheep don't like to make trouble.

Even as he watched this farce George was keenly aware of the horse's presence next to him in the small stall. He turned slowly to face him. George was immediately struck by just how "human" the horse was. His eyes showed the same gentle patience that he so often saw in Howie's. It was a type of tired recognition—a look that said this is the way that life is, so make the best of it. Such looks reflect a certain contentment, thought George, and also not just a little dullness. The horse brought his head very close as he looked at George. "I heard you last night—what you did for the squirrel—it was good that you were there." This surprised George and embarrassed him a little. Did the animals know and concern themselves with everything that went on in the house he wondered? But right now George was more curious about learning more about the dog, and he began questioning the horse. Whose dog was it? Why would it kill the squirrel if it didn't want to eat it?

"That dog is wild . . . belongs to no one . . . kills sometimes for food, but mostly for pleasure."

Kills for pleasure. The phrase sent shivers down George's spine. The horse seemed almost ashamed as he spoke of the dog, as if he took some of the responsibility on himself that any animal could be so wicked.

"There were chickens, once. The other people tried to raise them. Dog got them one by one—like it was a game. Men couldn't do nothing to stop it either."

George felt a sudden twinge of regret over the roach incidents in the city. But after all he had only been *playing.* The horse continued. "The dog's been roaming around here for years, and that's that." "But how does he get into the barn?" George asked. The horse shook his head gently from side to side. "He waits. Now that the spring is here we spend more and more time outside. Sometimes when it gets really hot we're left out all night too. In the warm weather that's when it's easy for the dog." The horse continued gravely. "In the winter we can hear him outside prowling, but we're protected. In the warm weather there's no defense except the man." The two animals exchanged a meaningful look. George tried to imagine how much help Howie would be in such a situation. "It was awful with the chickens, night after night, and me here in my stall. I couldn't do anything to help. All I could do was watch." The horse's voice became strained, as if he were again seeing the awful sights of those past nights.

It was at this point that Howie came to lead the horse outside. George decided not to follow. He had nothing to say, and wanted to be alone to think over what he had just heard.

He felt sorry for these animals. Big as they were, they were helpless. He would not trade places with them. Back at the house he curled up on the window ledge in the attic and, looking down on the sun-drenched barnyard where the animals were penned or tied or corralled, he dozed off thinking just that: he would never trade places with the animals in the barn.

His dreams, though, were far from sunny. They were clouded by the new realization that there were animals in the world that killed, animals that took lives not for food, which he could understand, but for fun. The dog killed senselessly, with no reason or excuse. George hated waste. It had something to do with his city upbringing. In the city nothing went to waste. Every square inch was important to someone or something. There was no spare anything. Everything was accounted for. Now, the country, on the other hand, was a place of waste. The space, the food growing and dying in the fields, the animals . . . the dog . . . No, the city was George's world, and maybe this house, but the rest was just not for him. And George dreamed on. . . .

After this first excursion, George remained very much a house cat, as he had been in the city and as his ancestors before him had been in cities all over the globe. In fact he became an attic cat. He loved the attic and spent most of his time up there. Howie began his new job and was gone all day. When he was home he was so busy with chores and other things that he never had to do in the city that George found himself almost always alone. He sat up in one of the attic windows sometimes, looking down on the animals, thinking that they certainly didn't lead much of a life.

They were either in the barn or out of the barn. The man moved them from place to place like pieces on a game board. Their lives had no particular purpose. They weren't supplying food, or helping with work or providing a source of money. They were just there. What possible pleasure could be derived from them? It seemed to be *all* work. But Howie seemed happy. George couldn't understand it, but he was happy for him. Toward the end there hadn't been all that much joy in their house in the city. But that was now in the past.

More of the time, George looked out of the front attic window. He watched the cars that infrequently passed on the little road out front. He was fascinated, also, to watch the trees fill out with leaves more and more every day. He even noticed a flower or two appear, and went down to the front porch to investigate. He liked keeping track of the changes, and tried to point them out to Howie, who seemed to pass them right by without noticing a thing was happening.

Sometimes he would lie out on the front porch when the man left in the morning. He would take up a position on top of the porch railing and wait for the sunshine to move across his space. Occasionally he would wander onto the lawn and play in the tall grass and weeds that grew at the base of the large oak trees. He missed the city very much, but he couldn't deny that it was nice having the house, and that it was especially fun to have the stairs and the attic. He loved to tear up several flights of stairs as fast as he could and make a playful swipe at the man as he passed him. He would howl the whole time. He could never have done that in the apartment. After his run he'd settle down in the sunlight and relax, reflecting that this life with Howie was *almost* as good as the city days.

Regardless of his mood, however, George was always a

conscientious cat. He was there to do his duty when he felt a need. He always offered sound advice, provided amusement when someone was sad or bored. Howie sensed that George was happy here, and listened as best he could to the endless stories of what George had seen in the attic or the yard. He didn't understand most of it, but he tried to be attentive and George was satisfied with the effort. Howie was too busy working to notice much of what George had the leisure to see and feel. So, each night George would meet Howie at the door and fill him in on what he'd missed that day. George felt it was his duty, and besides he missed the man a little when he wasn't around. George, of course, noticed everything—how the trees and the land and the house were all constantly changing. Every day there was a little alteration here and there, little details but constant motion. The man wasn't curious or inquisitive enough to discover these nuances without George's help.

In the city the sky was always changing, oh yes, and the trees too. But they were so far away that it seemed more of a sudden change. One minute they were green and the next multicolored on the way to becoming bare. Here all the movement was very subtle. George could almost feel the changes happening because he paid attention. The man didn't. Sometimes George wondered what Howie would do without him. He was lucky to have George to spot these things for him. George supposed that was one of the many reasons that the man took such good care of him, in appreciation.

This routine went on well into summer. The animals now spent their days almost entirely outdoors in the yard behind the house. George could hear their boring small talk, and smell their odors, made stronger by the heat, wherever he was sitting. They seemed to be content enough, for animals, and he began to enjoy watching them, especially in the moonlight. He was amazed to see them eating grass as if they enjoyed it. One day George tried to sample some—just to see—and had to force himself to have even a bite. Later he was quite sick. He was glad that Howie didn't try to make a uniform diet for all animals on the farm or there would have to be real trouble.

No way would he eat a plant again!

One Saturday Howie was painting the kitchen, one step in his long effort to renovate the house. The fumes permeated even the attic. George was bothered by the harsh smell even out on the front porch so he decided to go back into the barnyard where the animal smells would easily cover up any stray paint fumes that might drift back there. It had been many weeks since he had last been out to the barn, and George wasn't sure of what reception he would receive. He threw his head back defensively, lifted his tail straight up and walked

directly to the middle of the yard where the animals were, as usual, standing about in separate groups.

He inclined his head graciously in the horse's direction and looked haughtily over the heads of the goat and sheep as he gracefully jumped up onto the top plank of the split rail fence that surrounded the horse's paddock. George was instantly aware that the ram was afraid of him. He had lowered his head as if to attack and was noisily thumping the ground with his back hoof. Quite a show, thought George, but good luck if you think a little noise is going to scare me! The horse was quick to come over and greet George, calming the ram with his quiet and steady tone. "We haven't seen much of you lately. You haven't been sick have you?" he inquired of the cat. "It isn't often that we get new friends here and—" "Maybe he's your friend," snapped the goat. "But I'm surely not so desperate for visitors that I'll flatter every spoiled cat that happens to drift by." His head was held in a most self-satisfied tilt as he spoke, as if he were wearing a picture hat. "What's the good of a cat anyway?" he mused aloud. "Yes," broke in the sheep, in that annoying, bleating voice timid people use when they think they are being brave, "he can act as stuck up as he wants, but he's good for nothing and that's a fact."

"Good for—good for . . ." George had never heard such nonsense in his entire life. He cut the horse with a glance as it began to speak again, no doubt to make a conciliatory comment. "What's a cat good for?" He looked at each animal in turn, amazed. After a significant pause he answered.

Well, I guess I'm not good for much, I suppose. They can't keep me tied up here summer and winter to be fed and watered. People can't ride on me, or milk me or shear off my fur. No, I don't have to be led indoors and out, tended, nursed, bathed, fattened—and for what? What are you all "good for"? Oh, yes, for eating, and drinking, and pulling and carrying—but do you mean anything to anybody? Does the man love you, attend to what you say, come to you when he is lonely or hurt? Well, you may be right, I may not be "good for" much, but I wouldn't trade places with you domestic *animals [he almost hissed the word] for anything! A cat just is, and his just being there seems to mean more to people than the whole lot of you. A cat knows and sees and shares with its friends and nothing can buy that friendship. That's love given and freely returned. Maybe I don't do anything, but maybe I don't have to.*

The animals glared up at him silently. The ewe tossed her head. "Just as I thought," she whispered to the lambs, "wild— wild and good for nothing!" "Yep," repeated the ram, "wild like the birds, or the deer or the dog—the dog . . ." At this, even the horse looked over at George warily.

"Wild"—the idea had never entered his mind before, but compared with this pathetic lot he was wild and free, able to live his own life. The thought surprised him for a second, maybe even frightened him a little now that all the animals were staring up at him in that peculiar way. George tossed his head and was very careful to make his most graceful leap from the fence to the barnyard floor. He walked purposefully toward the house never turning back. He preferred some paint fumes to open hostility. But he was feeling less than self-assured. "Perhaps I'm not all that good after all," he mused.

That night George experienced unusual difficulty in find- ing just the right position for sleep. He finally snuggled close to Howie's leg on the bed, forming almost a perfect circle with his body head to tail. Some fanciful people believe that that's how the wheel was invented, by a man watching a cat sleep and being pleased by the perfect shape. But then you'll find men who believe almost anything.

George drifted off, and as he slept he dreamt. He was in a dark place, a room or forest where lights flickered far in the distance like reflections from far-off buildings. He was at the base of an enormous tree, green and fragrant. It was a huge fir, and as he lifted his head to try to see into its heights he narrowed his eyes to slits, sniffing and focusing his attention as all cats do with his ears stretching forward and his whiskers twitching with a life of their own. High above him in the tree he sensed movement and as he strained to make it clear he

began to see that the limbs were hung with the farm animals, as if this were an immense Christmas tree and they were the ornaments. Out of curiosity he began to climb, jumping easily from branch to branch until after a time he began to realize just how far away they really were. As he got closer he saw that these were not decorations above him but live animals. He even caught snatches of their conversations as they called to each other from branch to branch. Still climbing he began to reach the center of the tree and suddenly the animals above were cut off from his sight and he was only aware that something else had entered his dream. In the darkness at the heart of the tree, hidden from sight, he felt something much stronger and closer than the farm animals dangling so far above. He felt "another" very close by, and as he cautiously scanned the darkness he saw two bright points of yellow light glowing intensely just ahead of him. He knew they were the eyes of the dog, lurking in the darkness, waiting for him. And then he awoke.

For the next few days George spent as much time as he could with the man. Luckily the weather was rainy and they spent much of their time in the house. He stayed very close to Howie's side.

George had always been the man's companion, and in the next few weeks he became uniquely aware of that fact. He was free, but he chose the man as Howie had chosen him. He often remembered what the squirrel had said that night: "They are *your* animals. Protect your animals from the dog." He was companion to the man, owner of the farm, a part of the family. Yes, he liked the idea. As he sat on Howie's lap he thought about it, lifting his head so that Howie would scratch under his chin and be rewarded by a deep purr.

It was in this manner that George settled down to become his version of a country cat. The difference from his past life wasn't that great except that he spent so much of his time and energy taking note of things perhaps because there was so much more here to take note of. He spent hours in the attic or in the yards or in front of the fireplace, because even though it was summer many of the nights were still cold. Well, they weren't *that* cool but it made Howie feel more countrified to always have a fire in the fireplace at night so George got to enjoy this treat all the time.

Howie was beginning to entertain now, since he had gotten the farm "together," as he called it. All week George had the house to himself, but on weekends there were often several friends who arrived from the city. George did his best to help with the entertaining, and he would personally point out what he felt were the farm's best features. Many of Howie's friends brought him special treats from this or that famous deli, things that were known to be his favorites. That was nice, and it again proved that he was part of the family. He couldn't imagine anyone bringing treats for a sheep or a goat. Everybody recognized that he was family and treated him accordingly. But even with this increased company George spent most of his time alone and he grew to like it more and more. He was especially happy in the attic. There he could hear and feel the house better than anywhere else. He heard it talk as it settled and groaned, drying out the winter dampness and expanding in the spring warmth. George imagined he was on a great ship transporting them through the seasons. In the attic he heard and felt it all, and it was also here that he would occasionally look at the dark stain of dried blood on the flooring and remember the squirrel and the truth that life

wasn't always as simple as it appeared.

So the days passed and George began to settle in, much as the old house did, with the rhythm of the seasons and the passing of the years. Summer progressed and George gloried in the intense warmth and sunlight and the activity of nature on all sides. But right at the height of summer, he began to notice little signs that hinted fall was already approaching. Slowly of course, but there were changes already in motion. Nothing stayed the same for long in nature, and that notion appealed to George. He began to imagine what the farm would be like in the fall with its leaves of all colors. Now when he went outdoors, he saw himself playing with leaves as they spiraled from the trees on their way to forming thick beds on the lawn. He'd hide behind something, waiting for a leaf to fall, and then dart out and catch it up in his paws, falling over and over himself in the soft piles of leaves that were everywhere. He went over these games repeatedly in his mind as he looked out the window at the trees covered with strong, green leaves, feeling the subtle stir of change in the air. *Spring* and *fall*—the words themselves described what nature was doing out there in the world and George was fascinated to watch each little step and phase.

His days continued in this manner. A cat's life is rarely exciting you know. Full, because of all the things that have to be watched and checked out and studied, but not exciting. We tend not to realize just how much a cat does because he does it all so effortlessly. For instance, to watch George as he sat in the attic window intently gazing at the trees, you'd never guess that he was monitoring the season's progress, making sure that things were advancing properly. If that weren't important enough there was the house to look after and Howie to be cared for, and yet he did it all so quietly and easily that if you weren't *very* observant you'd think that he spent the whole day dozing in the sun.

George, like all cats, was really a guest in the man's house and like any good guest he tried to make himself useful in small ways, at the same time not drawing attention to himself. Cats are the perfect guests. George was thinking on these very matters one day when he realized that yes, perhaps the animals had been right. He was *wild*, if that meant free. "I'm not only wild, I'm happy to be." And at this he lashed his tail viciously a few times, but it was strictly for emphasis.

Somehow it took a few days before George registered the unmistakable signs that a trip was in the air. It wasn't until Howie actually started packing an overnight bag and setting out several dishes of water and dry food that George was really certain. Howie hadn't gone anywhere in so long, that the whole thing came as quite a surprise to George. In the city, Howie spent many weekends away at the beach in summer, visiting friends, or skiing in the winter. At these times George had the whole apartment to himself which he, of course, liked. Since they had come to the farm, people came to visit them and the man stayed put. George became excited at the thought of having *this house* all to himself and actually began to look forward to it. Just before the man left, the girl arrived. She was a teenager who lived on a neighboring farm, a real farm, where hard work was a way of life. Shortly after the move she had come over to offer to help out and since then she came over most weekends, often driving pieces of heavy farm machinery that made keeping the fields cut easy. Tonight, she was only there to feed and water the animals who, since it was a particularly hot night, were out in the barnyard. After she was done she came into the house to check on George. Smiling at the line of plates and bowls that had been left out, she stroked the cat absently on the head. George was especially interested in the fact that she had brought along her dog—Carl. George had often seen him from a distance running through the fields chasing after the girl on the tractor. He looked so strong and happy that George had been intrigued by him. Carl looked a little shy and out of place in the kitchen, as if being indoors were a new and not particularly pleasing experience. He walked over to George thumping his heavy tail against the legs of the kitchen table. For a moment they looked at each other and then Carl plopped down on his front paws raising up his tail and proceeded to laugh and laugh. "What a scrawny excuse for a cat you are," he guffawed. "I'd like to see you face-to-face with one of the barn rats at our place," and he beat the floor with his large paws in uncontrollable laughter at the very idea of such an encounter. George just looked steadily at the dog. Absently he noticed how the dog's tail was sweeping against the water bowls and making a puddle on the kitchen floor.

No surprise you don't get into the house much, thought George as he turned and pushed open the swinging door into the living room.

The girl gave Carl a swat and herded him toward the door. She had the country attitude toward animals—took them for granted the way city people do elevators or streetlights. They were a part of her everyday world and she barely noticed them, except for the work they required of her. It amused her to see the fuss Howie made over George.

After Carl and the girl were gone, George went on a full house inspection. He reviewed all the changes that had been made since that day months ago when they had first moved there. It was really a home now, their home and every bit as comfortable as the apartment had been though less exciting. George liked the smell and the space of this house. It was "warm"—that's what all the weekend guests said, and George heartily agreed with them. "Warm" was the best word to describe the farm.

After he had completed his inspection the problem arose of where he would sleep that night. He could lie on a bed, or burrow under the covers, which he sometimes did when he was alone. Better yet, he'd go up into the attic and sleep in the pool of moonlight that he knew waited on the back sill.

From up here where he lay the yard was fully visible and George gazed out at the scene as he had once looked out over the streets and buildings of the city. He looked toward the animals and couldn't help wondering if they should be out with no one around. But the girl had watered and fed them and she was a "farm girl," so she should know what was right in these matters. She certainly had to know more than Howie, who was constantly on the phone or dropping by neighbors' farms to get advice or explanations. He was still a long way from knowing his way around in the country.

The sheep were huddled together in their pen near the big tree, and the goat lay next to the post where he was tied. The horse looked over them all from his paddock. George thought that he saw the horse look up toward the attic, where he lay; but since horses are always raising and lowering their heads it was hard to be certain. In the darkness of the attic, with just a ray or two of moonlight, George began to doze.

As he slept he dreamt of the city and its skyline and the times he was a kitten and lay in the warm sun looking over the park with the sun and shadows. As the sky darkened you began to see the lights come on, one by one. The buildings seemed to be taking new shapes as the darkness erased the stone, and all the separate lights in the millions of windows formed new buildings that were really one big splash of light that stretched across the city as far as the eye could see. At the heart of that picture was the park, cool and green in summer, gray and mysterious in winter, but always dark and deep compared with the solid light that surrounded it. He loved the sight of the moon rising over all of this and the sounds of the street that he could hear as a whisper so far, far off . . . sounds—sounds. He awoke suddenly. It was very bright now, for the moon had risen to its fullness, and it lit up the evening world. The animals were still lost in sleep—but George heard or sensed something, and then he actually saw it. He was immediately sure what it was. Far back, just at the edge of the field, with the moonlight framing it, was the dog. It was big, almost as large as the ram, but with none of that bulkiness. No, the dog was strong and well muscled—sleek, like George. George was afraid. The animals were outside and the dog had finally come. Howie was away and the dog had come. What could *he* do? He couldn't even warn Howie or the animals that the dog was here—the dog. He shuddered as his gaze involuntarily shifted to the dark spot on the boards where the squirrel had died. That spot was the dog—that wound in the squirrel's chest—that was the dog.

As he watched, the dog crept slowly, leisurely along the border of the field to where the underbrush ran close to the barnyard. It was a game to him, there was no fear. He knew that he had no enemies worthy of the name, at least not here.

Quietly, very quietly, the dog came closer. Looking out from the window, George felt like the spectator that he always was, but this time he knew that more was required of him. George realized that *he* had to do something, that there was no man, only him. What could he do, a cat, a wild animal? He could almost hear the goat and ram saying it: "wild animal . . . wild . . . wild . . ." The repetition in his mind went on, became a chant. His eyes closed and the wildness enveloped him. "*Wild . . . wild . . .*" The words beat to the rhythm of his heart which he felt pounding in his ears.

> *Wild . . . Wild*
> *Blood of the Cheetah*
> *Blood of the Leopard*
> *Blood of the Panther*
> *Blood of the Lion*

Blood of the Tiger
Wild . . .

The chant ran on through his veins as if it were an essential, ancient part of him. He had never been aware of it before, but he recognized it now and it held his mind with its life. He felt the power in his blood for what it really was, the power he shared with these other "wild" ones. The chant continued and gained in volume, over and over it ran as George made his way from the attic, through the house and toward the yard. He walked fluidly as if the air around him were water and he was king of the sea.

In a second he was at the back door, his tail lashing, his head cocked and watchful. The dog was already in the yard and the animals, now aware of their danger, were frozen with the realization that they were tied and vulnerable. Even an attempt at flight was impossible.

In their pen the sheep huddled in the farthest corner, while the dog stalked the lamb, who stood unsteadily and alone in the center of the small enclosed space. The dog's gaze jerked away from the frightened lamb to throw a warning glare to the other animals. Then he stared at the lamb, almost hypnotizing it with his look of control and self-assurance.

George leapt up to an open window in the kitchen and out into the yard. His eyes blazed with grim determination as he too stalked toward the pen—a second predator had arrived. His heartbeat continued to throb in his ears, as if his every move were being accompanied both by a drum and the chanting of the inner voice. He circled the pen, away from the dog, and in one powerful leap he cleared the fence and landed on the ram's back. "Listen to me," he hissed in the terrified

animal's ear. "We're going to save the lamb, and you will do *exactly* what I say." With that he dug his claws slightly into either side of the ram's neck to emphasize his point. "I can't," bleated the ram. "You will," George hissed, and he again dug his claws into the ram. The present pain seemed to frighten the animal even more than the thought of the approaching dog. "Do what I tell you." And George felt that the ram was now ready to comply.

The dog was slinking closer to the spot where the lamb stood totally immobilized by fear. At George's urging the ram began to paw at the ground furiously. Lowering its head he charged the dog. Unconcerned, the dog shifted his gaze and raised his head, baring his fangs. It all took a split second. At the very last instant, the ram veered sharply and hit the dog not head on, but full force to his side, knocking him off balance. At the same instant George leapt from the ram's back and lunged for the dog's throat.

There was no time for thinking. It was as if he had always known precisely what to do. He remained calm and sure. When he felt enough damage had been done, he left the dog and jumped to the barnyard fence. All the time his tail was inflated and lashing violently with its own life, as if a powerful snake had been freed. His face, however, appeared calm though his eyes burned a little too bright. The dog never stopped howling. Now that he had the chance he fled from the pen, through the barnyard toward the woods. There was no doubt that he was badly hurt, and an animal wants to be alone at such a time.

From his place on the fence George looked back on the animals. He inspected to see if they were all right. The entire time his tail continued to lash and his eyes darted restlessly about. He was still ready for anything and the beat of his inner voice continued to sound clearly in his ears. But there was no more danger, and all he saw were the animals looking up at him blankly with a mix of wonder and fear. They had seen that he really was wild—but that didn't help them understand him any more than they had before. Livestock, he thought. The name all of a sudden had real meaning. Just "play things," *they* were really man's toys.

He strode back to the house. The voice within him was ebbing slowly away. He would wait up for the man's return next morning. He would be right there to greet him because he loved him. Howie, he felt, had always known about the wildness. He could understand it and love him because of it. The man loved him because George shared with him, and gave him joy. Howie understood the privilege of having a wild thing willingly sharing itself and its life with him for no other reason but love.

George curled up in the attic window facing the front of the house. He would wait up through the rest of the night for Howie. He sat at the window cleaning himself, thinking of the man, and the squirrel and the dog. But mostly he thought about the man. How anxious he was for him to return so they could be together, so that Howie would play with him and call him "tiger."